This book belongs to

....

First published in 2019 by Miles Kelly Publishing Ltd
Harding's Barn, Bardfield End Green, Thaxted, Essex, CM6 3PX, UK

Copyright © Miles Kelly Publishing Ltd 2019

2·4 6 8 10 9 7 5 3 1

Publishing Director Belinda Gallagher
Creative Director Jo Cowan
Editorial Director Rosie Neave
Senior Editor Fran Bromage
Senior Designer Rob Hale
Image Manager Liberty Newton
Production Elizabeth Collins, Jennifer Brunwin-Jones
Reprographics Stephan Davis, Callum Ratcliffe-Bingham
Assets Lorraine King

Cover Ailie Busby at The Bright Agency

ISBN 978-1-78617-862-6

Printed in China

British Library Cataloguing-in-Publication Data
A catalogue record for this book is available from the British Library

Made with paper from a sustainable forest

www.mileskelly.net

My First Book of
Dinosaur Stories

Written by Catherine Veitch
and Fran Bromage

MILES KELLY

Contents

T rex

The big scare

Say hello to the dinosaurs in this story!

Tyrannosaurus rex
(say *tie-RAN-oh-sore-us rex*)

Troodon
(say *TROH-oh-don*)

Triceratops
(say *tri-SERRA-tops*)

Parasaurolophus
(say *pa-ra-saw-ROL-oh-fus*)

Long, long ago there lived a
dinosaur called Rex.
"When I grow up, I'm going
to be the biggest, scariest,
noisiest dinosaur ever,"
he roared. "I'll be
just like my
mum, and

RRROO

we're not afraid of anything!"
said the little Tyrannosaurus rex.

AAARRR!

Rex didn't have many friends. He was just too big, too scary, and too noisy to play with.

GULP!

One day Rex was stomping through the forest when he scared a Troodon called Travis.

"Aah! Don't DO that, Rex!"
cried Travis.
"I can do what I want,"
roared Rex. "I'm going to be the
biggest, scariest, noisiest
dinosaur ever!"

RRROOOAAARRR!

Next, Rex scared old Trudi Triceratops who was quietly eating leaves. "Aah!" cried Trudi. "Stop doing that Rex!"

PRROOOAAARRR!

"I'm not afraid of anything!" replied Rex. "I'm going to be the biggest, scariest, noisiest dinosaur ever!"

Everyone was very tired of
Rex scaring them. So, the next
day Travis and the other
Troodons came up with a plan.
Travis found Rex in
the forest and said,

"You won't be the biggest dinosaur ever. My dad says there are lots of dinosaurs bigger than you."

Rex was furious! So he chased after Travis, roaring loudly.

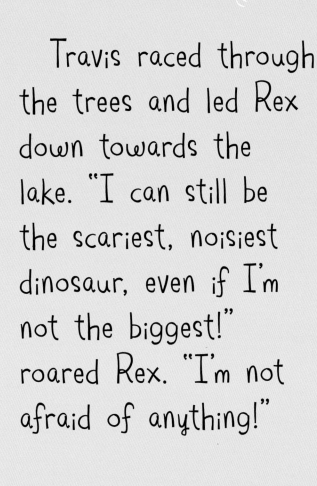

Travis raced through
the trees and led Rex
down towards the
lake. "I can still be
the scariest, noisiest
dinosaur, even if I'm
not the biggest!"
roared Rex. "I'm not
afraid of anything!"

19

Rex skidded
to a halt by a group of
Troodons who were
gathered in a circle.
"Look what we found,"
they said, showing Rex
some bright white things.

"What ARE they?" whispered Rex. The bright white things were flowers, but not many dinosaurs had ever seen them before. Suddenly, a low humming

BBBUZZZZ!

sound came from inside one of the flowers. "Aaahhh!" bellowed Rex, backing away.

"Buzzzz, buzz!" said the flower again, and Rex ran shrieking into the trees.

"Look!" said Travis. "It's just a little stripy thing," and a buzzy bee crawled out of the flower.

"Rex was so scared! We're not afraid of him now," laughed the Troodons.

BBBUZZZZ!

But Rex
was too far
away to hear
them. He ran and ran and ran
until he found Trudi Triceratops.
Rex told Trudi all about the
buzzing white things.

So Trudi decided to go to the
lake and see for herself.

Rex watched from behind a rock as Trudi walked closer to the lake, the white flowers and the stripy buzzing things.

"Aaah, these are flowers!" said the wise, old Triceratops.

"You'll see many more of these as the world begins to change. And these buzzy things are bees. They help the flowers to grow. There's nothing scary here," said Trudi.

BBBUZZZZ!

29

Rex sat quietly on a rock
looking around him.
  "But I WAS scared," said Rex
to himself. "And I'm not
supposed to be afraid
of anything!"

"Yeah!" shouted Travis popping up behind Rex. "Terrible Rex is scared of flowers. Ha, ha!"

"Everyone is scared of something," said Trudi. "But it isn't nice to be teased about it."

"Rex teased us all the time," replied Travis. "And he was always scaring us with his roaring."

Suddenly, a deafening noise rocked the lake. It sounded just like a giant horn! "Waaaaaaaaah! What was that?" cried Travis, as he leaped into Rex's arms.

BBBWWWAAARRR!

Seconds later, Piper the
Parasaurolophus appeared out of
the water and blew her head
crest again.

"Ha, ha! It's only Piper,"

BBBWWWAAARRR!

laughed Rex putting Travis down. "You were really scared."

"So were you!" shouted Travis over the noise. "But everyone's scared of something!"

"So I'll never be the biggest, scariest or noisiest dinosaur," sighed Rex. "I'm scared of flowers, bees and loud noises!"

"But Rex, we like you even more because of that!" said the others, and everyone laughed.

Psittacosaurus

The lost egg

Say hello to the dinosaurs in this story!

Psittacosaurus
(say *SIT-uh-koh-sore-us*)

Tenontosaurus
(say *ten-ON-toe-sore-us*)

Austrosaurus
(say *oss-TROH-sore-us*)

Baryonyx
(say *bah-ree-ON-icks*)

Also featuring: Ornithocheirus (say *OR-nith-o-kee-rus*)

A long, long time ago Sid, a Psittacosaurus, was sleeping in his burrow. Suddenly a fiery volcano exploded.

It blasted hot rocks, ash and... an egg high into the air. The egg bounced into Sid's burrow and hit him on the head!

BOING!

"Where have you come from little egg?" said Sid, rubbing his sore head.

But the egg didn't answer. So Sid made up his mind to try to find who it belonged to.

41

Sid gently picked up
the egg in his mouth
and crept out of his
burrow.

It wasn't
easy scrambling
over the beach with
an egg in his mouth.

Sid wondered where to start
looking for the egg's home.
Suddenly an Ornithocheirus
swooped down from the sky and,

quick as a flash, knocked the
egg out of Sid's beak. "Hey!
Watch where you're going,
clumsy!" shouted Sid.

The egg sailed
through the air.

It bounced and rolled away from Sid, who ran after it yelling, "Stop little egg! Stop!"

But the egg carried
on rolling until...

...it bumped into an enormous, scaly foot. Sid ran straight into the foot too and plonked down next to the egg.

"Er, is this your egg?" Sid asked, staring up at an enormous Austrosaurus.

"That tiny egg would never belong to me!" laughed the Austrosaurus. "Make sure it gets home safely though won't you?"

Sid grabbed the egg in his mouth and hurried out of the forest. But he ran into a swarm

BZZZZZZZZZZ!

of flying ants. They buzzed loudly as they flew past Sid's ear.

Sid shrieked and dropped the egg again.

The egg bounced away from
Sid again, who ran after it
yelling, "Stop little egg! Stop!"
But it didn't stop until it hit the
big nose of a Tenontosaurus.

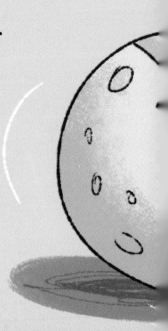

Sid crawled into the ferns to get the egg. "Is this yours?" he asked Theo the Tenontosaurus.

"I'm far too big to have an egg that

small!" chuckled Theo. "Be gentle with it and get it home safely."

59

Sid picked up the egg and hurried away, but he wasn't looking where he was going...

...and fell into a huge hole.

"Argh!" he shouted, and once more the egg fell out of his mouth. "Come back little egg!

Come back!"
Sid cried.

The egg bounced away again. Sid ran after it yelling, "Stop little egg! Stop!" But it didn't stop until it was caught in the enormous mouth of a Baryonyx.

63

"I came here for fish, not an egg!" snapped Bella the Baryonyx, spitting out the egg. "You're scaring away the fish! Be off with you."

Sid grabbed the egg and ran away from the river.

He jumped back over the hole and scrambled through the ferns.

He dodged around the flying ants
and scurried through the forest.

He ducked past the
Ornithocheirus and staggered
along the beach.

Finally Sid reached his home. "I'm sorry little egg," said Sid, sadly. "I couldn't find your home."

Suddenly, there was a loud CRACK and a little beak peeped

out from a small hole in the egg.
Then a head and two arms
appeared, before a whole baby
dinosaur popped out of the egg!

The baby dinosaur looked just like Sid! "Say hello to your baby sister," said Sid's daddy.

"Oh!" said Sid. "You naughty little egg, you belonged here all along!" and everyone laughed.

Diplodocus

The dippy idea

Say hello to the dinosaurs in this story!

Diplodocus
(say *DIP-low-DOKE-cus*)

Allosaurus
(say *AL-oh-SORE-us*)

Stegosaurus
(say *STEG-oh-SORE-us*)

Ornitholestes
(say *Or-nith-oh-LES-teez*)

Also featuring: Plesiosaurus (say *ples-EE-oh-sore-rus*)

There was once a huge and
hungry Diplodocus called
Dora. Dora often had lots of
dippy ideas and was very easily
confused.

'Hmm... the best leaves are on that side of the tree,' she thought, one day. 'So if I stand here, I can twist my neck round like this to reach them!'

"Dora! You nearly stepped on me!" shouted a small Ornitholestes. "Head over there will you?"

"But my head IS over there," Dora replied, confused.

But before Dora could move away, an old Diplodocus appeared through the trees.
"Sssh! There's an Allosaurus about!" he hissed.

Dora made herself as small as possible and hid behind the nearest tree. From there she watched as the herd swung their

enormous necks and tails at the group of Allosaurus to try to scare them off.

After the fight everyone was hungry, but they also wanted to think of new ways to scare off the Allosaurus. The Diplodocus were tired of all the neck-swinging

80

and having their meals interrupted. "We could disguise ourselves... as trees," suggested Dora, "with leaves on our heads!"

81

But no one took Dora seriously, so she wandered off on her own.

Deeper in the forest, Dora spotted a Stegosaurus frightening off another Allosaurus.

"You did it!"
said Dora, strolling
over to the smiling
Stegosaurus called Peggy.
"I wish I had super strong
plates on my back," Dora sighed.

Peggy helped Dora make her own plates with mud and leaves.

"This is a great idea!" smiled Dora. "We'll all look so super-fierce. No Allosaurus will dare to come near us!"

But everyone laughed at Dora's idea and went back to eating leaves.

Poor Dora felt sad as she wandered down to the rocky shore to wash off her disguise.

"Never mind," said Peggy.
"You'll think of something else."
"Er, Peggy?" whispered Dora.
"What's that in the water?"

Dora plunged
her head into the
water and looked about.
"Who's in here?" she tried to say
underwater (but it came out a
little like "blooob-bo-ber?").

"I'm Pete. I'm a Plesiosaurus. Are you coming in for a swim?"

Dora thought for a moment. She wasn't even sure Diplodocus COULD swim!

"Try it and see," said Pete.
So Dora found some hollow
reeds to help her breathe under
the water and dived right in!
'Wow, what a good way to

hide,' thought Dora. 'My whole herd could fit down here.'

"And there's food!"
said Dora, trying a big
clump of seaweed.

She didn't see the
Allosaurus had returned.
And she didn't see
Peggy at the edge of
the shore trying to
warn her.

"Peggy! I've got the best idea," said Dora. "I think we should... Wooooaaah!"

As Dora staggered out of the sea, she slid into a huge puddle of mud. She was covered in thick, drippy black slime. The reeds, leaves and seaweed stuck out at

all angles. The Allosaurus had
never seen anything so terrifying
in all their lives!

101

"Well done Dora!"
said the Diplodocus
herd. "This dippy
idea wasn't so silly
after all!"

Spinosaurus

The roaring river

Say hello to the dinosaurs in this story!

Spinosaurus
(say *SPY-noh-SORE-us*)

Avimimus
(say *ah-vee-MEE-mus*)

Bambiraptor
(say *bam-BEE-rap-tor*)

Bagaceratops
(say *bag-a-SERRA-tops*)

Suki was the new dinosaur in the valley. She lived near a roaring river with her mum and dad. With her huge sail, big snout and long claws, Suki

looked fierce. But all she wanted was to make some friends.

The other dinosaurs were afraid of Suki, and this made her sad and lonely.

One day Suki went for a walk through the valley. She spotted a little Bambiraptor who looked like she would make a good friend. "Hello," she said. "I'm Suki, I'm new here."

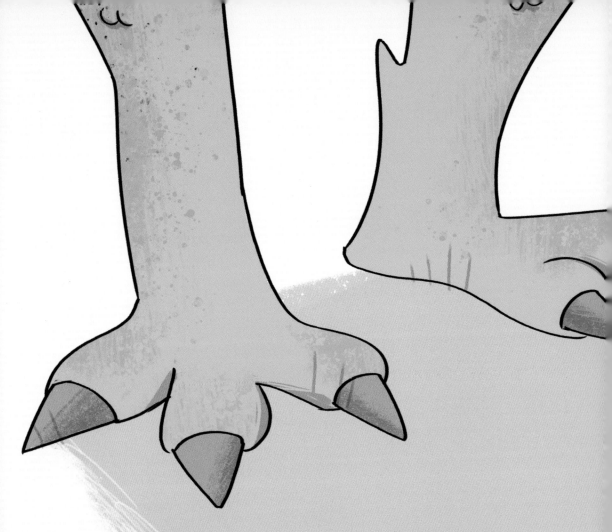

But Suki's sail cast a
huge shadow over the little
Bambiraptor, whose name
was Beth.

She was so frightened that she ran off without even saying her name.

Next, Suki came across a little Bagaceratops chomping on grass. A bird had landed on his bottom!

"Excuse me, you have a bird on your bottom!" laughed Suki.

The Bagaceratops,
whose name was Billy,
turned around and
had the fright of
his life...

HAHAHA!

...Suki's huge jaws were wide open as she roared with laughter. Billy plodded away as fast as he could.

On her way home Suki spotted an Avimimus. 'I'll try to make a friend one last time,' she thought.

Suki waved. But the Avimimus, whose name was Amy, took one look at Suki's razor-sharp claws and ran off.

At home, Suki felt sad. "Why are you so sad?" asked her mum. "No one wants to be my friend because they're scared of me," said Suki.

"Give them time to get to
know you," said her mum.
"Then, they'll see how lovely
you are and they won't be
scared anymore."

Suki felt happier after talking to her mum. She ran off to find the other dinosaurs.

Beth, Billy and Amy were playing by the roaring river, so Suki went over to say a proper hello.

The river suddenly
burst its banks and
water crashed over the
young dinosaurs.
"HELP!" they yelled
to Suki.

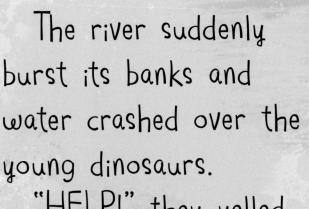

Suki staggered to her feet. She was just big enough to stand up in the water. But the little dinosaurs were not so lucky. The raging river tossed

and jostled them, and carried
them downstream.
"HELP!" they all screamed.
"I'm coming!" shouted Suki.

Beth was nearest to Suki. She
bravely clung to a tree root.
Suki struggled against the
water and waded over to Beth.

"Climb up my sail and hold on tight," Suki said gently. And she helped Beth onto her sail.

129

Further upstream,
Billy clung to a log.
Suki pushed against
the current to get to
him. It was harder
now with Beth on
her back.

131

"Keep still, don't
be scared," Suki
told Billy when
she reached him.
Then she carefully
picked him up in her
huge jaws and held him
above the water.

A long way upstream Amy was sprawled on a rock. The river was swirling around Suki.

It was hard carrying
both Beth and Billy.

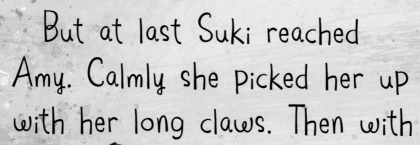

But at last Suki reached
Amy. Calmly she picked her up
with her long claws. Then with

all three little dinosaurs
safely in her care,
Suki waded to
the bank.

137

The dinosaurs' families were all waiting on the bank. They were so happy to see Suki and the

little dinosaurs safely reach dry land.

"You're a real friend now," said Suki's mum with a smile. "But find a safer place to play away from the river."

139

The dinosaurs in the valley weren't afraid of Suki anymore. And Suki loved her brand new friends!

Ankylosaurus

The clumsy club

Say hello to the dinosaurs in this story!

Ankylosaurus
(say *an-KIE-loh-sore-us*)

Ornithomimus
(say *or-NITH-oh-MEE-mus*)

Styracosaurus
(say *sty-RAK-oh-sore-us*)

Tyrannosaurus rex
(say *tie-RAN-oh-sore-us rex*)

Once upon a time, a long time
ago, there was a young
Ankylosaurus called Archie.
Archie was a tough-looking

dinosaur, but he was ever so shy and ever so clumsy.

Archie had a huge club at the end of his tail. It seemed to do the exact opposite of what he wanted it to do.

Poor Archie often destroyed things just by wandering past them, because when he walked, his club swiped from side to side.

So Archie spent a lot of time saying sorry to other dinosaurs. His club was always getting him into trouble.

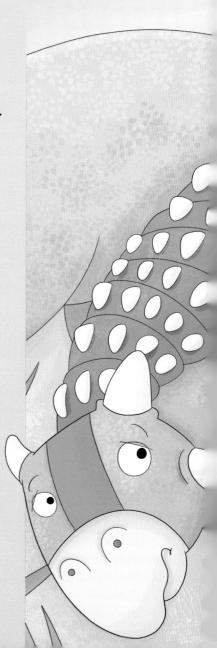

SMASH!

145

"Watch your club!"
grumbled an old
        Edmontonia.
    "I don't know
    why you've
    got a tail club,

146

if you can't control it."
   But poor Archie was still
learning what his club
could do.

Archie's best friend was a Styracosaurus called Stu. Archie and Stu had lots of fun playing together. But even with Stu sticking up for him, Archie was still left out of games — he was just too clumsy.

149

"Stu! Come and play hide and seek," shouted an Ornithomimus called Olivia, one day.

"HE can't
play though," added
Olivia, pointing to
Archie. "He'll knock half the
forest down before we've had
time to hide."

It made Archie feel sad, but
he told Stu to go and play with
everyone anyway.

Archie stood and watched as
all the other dinosaurs ran off

to hide in different
places in the forest.

"Can I at least help you find
them?" Archie asked Olivia, as
he lumbered up to her.

"Ssshh... 18, 19, 20. Coming!" she shouted.
"Oh, I suppose so," she replied, "just try to be quiet."

Olivia and Archie started
hunting for the other dinosaurs.
But suddenly Archie spotted a
dinosaur who wasn't part of
their game.

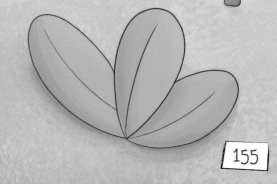

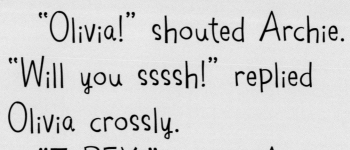

"Olivia!" shouted Archie. "Will you ssssh!" replied Olivia crossly.

"T REX!" hissed Archie.

"What?!" shrieked Olivia. "T REEEEEX!" she screamed, as she overtook Archie and sped towards a nearby cave.

Archie could see the other dinosaurs already hiding in the cave.

Stu was waiting for him, but was Archie

going to get there in time? Just
as he got to the cave there was
a thundering roar and the
ground began to shake.

Archie wondered what he'd hit with his club this time. When he looked behind him the sky was filling with smoke.

A huge, rumbling volcano
shot fiery balls of lava into the
air, and Archie still hadn't
reached the cave.

Everyone else ducked inside
just as an enormous rockfall
filled the cave entrance.

Rocks, bits of tree and hot
ash fell from the sky and
bounced off Archie's hard
armoured body.

Archie huddled close to the cave as the eruption continued.

He swiped hot lava away with his tail club and as the eruption calmed, Archie began pushing at the rocks blocking the cave.

"I — can't — shift — any of them," he grunted.

"Try harder!" shouted
Stu from inside the cave.
"We've been trying to move rocks
from inside here, but we can only
move the little ones."

164

Olivia squeezed her
head through the small gap
Stu was making from the outside.

"Archie!" called Olivia. "Now would be a great time to use your club," she suggested.

"No! I'll hurt someone," said Archie. "I always break something with it."

"You'll be fine — just give it a swipe and see which rocks you can move. But hurry Archie!" shouted Olivia. "T rex is back!"

"Just give your tail a swish and try. Please?" called Stu.

So Archie flicked his tail from side to side and a few rocks fell from around the cave entrance. He swiped one way, then the other. Finally, Archie started to spin and his club slammed into the fallen rocks.

As T rex got closer, small trees and boulders were caught up in Archie's whirling.

169

Archie spun faster and faster
until T rex, trying to dodge the

WHOOOSH!

debris, was
hit by a large
flying branch.

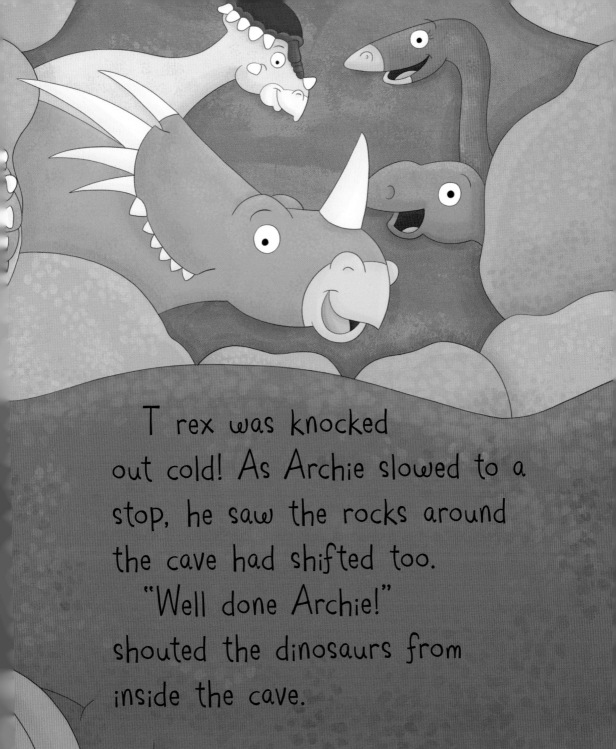

T rex was knocked
out cold! As Archie slowed to a
stop, he saw the rocks around
the cave had shifted too.
    "Well done Archie!"
shouted the dinosaurs from
inside the cave.

"Thanks Archie," whispered
each dinosaur as they tiptoed
over T rex to leave the cave.
"You took on a T rex with

your tail?" whispered a small Edmontonia. "Amazing!"

Archie felt enormously proud of his tail club.

Archie was soon part of everyone's games and found he was especially good at rock-ball! "Archie — your club really is awesome!" laughed Olivia.

Plateosaurus
The selfish dinosaur

Say hello to the dinosaurs in this story!

Plateosaurus
(say *pla-tee-oh-SORE-us*)

Eoraptor
(say *EE-oh-RAP-tor*)

Melanorosaurus
(say *mela-nor-oh-SORE-us*)

Coelophysis
(say *see-LOH-fie-sis*)

Also featuring: Euskelosaurus (say *yoo-SKEL-uh-SORE-us*)

A young Plateosaurus called Posy once lived near a dusty desert. She had the best spot beside a river.

Posy was a selfish dinosaur. If she found her favourite liverwort leaves growing nearby,

she wouldn't tell her friends.
"There's no liverwort here,"
she would say, and send them
looking in the opposite direction.

Every day, Posy played rock skittles. There was always a queue of other dinosaurs waiting to play. But Posy wouldn't share.

Once, a brave little Eoraptor called Esme dared to

ask for a turn in her BIGGEST
voice. "Please can I play?"
      Posy held on tight to her
rock and said, "No, you
      can't play! These
      are MY skittles!
      Go away!"

181

Each day, dinosaurs had to cross a bridge over the river to reach the shady trees on the other side.

Posy wouldn't let them cross. She said, "This is MY bridge and you can't cross here." So all the dinosaurs had to go the longer way round.

WAAAHH!

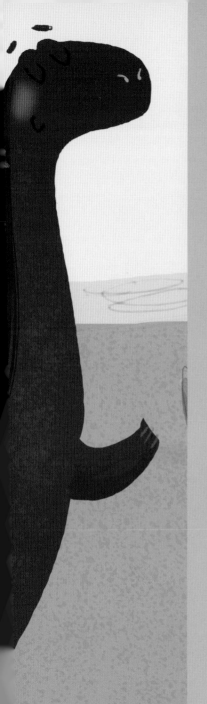

Things carried on like this until a new dinosaur moved into the desert. The new dinosaur's name was Malik and he was a Melanorosaurus. And Malik was just as selfish as Posy.

One hot day,
Malik started to
cross the bridge to
reach the shady side
of the river.

"Get off MY bridge!"
shouted Posy.
"It's MY bridge
now!" shouted Malik.

The other dinosaurs suggested that Posy and Malik have a competition. The winner of the competition would be the

owner of the bridge.
First they had a race.

"And the winner is, Posy!"
shouted Esme. "I won, I'm the
winner!" cried Posy. "It's my
bridge!"

Next there was a log-lifting contest to see who was the strongest. Posy gripped a log in her jaws and heaved it in the air.

But Malik hauled an even bigger log higher than Posy did. "Malik is the winner!" shouted Charlie the Coelophysis.

193

"Who can jump the highest?" asked Esme. Posy and Malik both leapt into the air at the same time. Esme and Charlie measured their jumps.

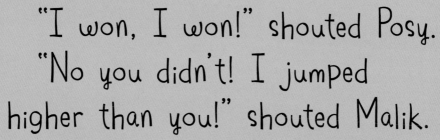

"I won, I won!" shouted Posy.
"No you didn't! I jumped
higher than you!" shouted Malik.
There was a
hush as the
winner was
announced...

"It's... a draw!"
said Charlie.

196

Posy and Malik had both won. They were too surprised to speak!

But Posy and Malik didn't
like being winners together.
They didn't want to share
the bridge.
    They argued long into the
afternoon. Suddenly everyone
heard a loud, "ROAR!"

Then from the forest came a huge, stomping, roaring beast. It marched towards the bridge. "It's a Euskelosaurus! RUUUN!" shouted Posy and Malik.

RAAA!

There was a crazy bundle as the little dinosaurs sped off.

Posy and Malik stood side-by-side on the bridge. "No one is crossing OUR bridge!" they said. They rose onto their back legs

and bared their teeth and claws.
The Euskelosaurus stopped in
its tracks...

"Get off OUR bridge!"
shouted Posy and Malik
together.

Posy and Malik's plan worked! The Euskelosaurus turned its back and slunk away into the forest.

"He won't dare step on OUR bridge again!" they laughed.

Everyone heard how Posy and Malik worked together to scare away the Euskelosaurus.

"Has the mean dinosaur really gone?" asked Esme.

"Yes, and it's not coming back," smiled Posy.

"It's more fun doing things together," Posy said. Malik agreed,

and from then on they shared the bridge with everyone.

Velociraptor

The speedy tale

Say hello to the dinosaurs in this story!

Velociraptor
(say ve-LOSS-ee-rap-tor)

Protoceratops
(say pro-toe-SERRA-tops)

Gallimimus
(say gal-lee-MEE-mus)

Tarbosaurus
(say TAR-bow-SORE-us)

Millions of years ago, there lived a Velociraptor called Vicky, who was super-speedy. Everywhere she went, she went in a rush.

"Got to go! Can't stop!" she'd shout, ignoring her baby brothers and sisters as she rushed past them.

Vicky ran this way...

...then she raced that way...

...and then she sped back again.

When Vicky's
family was
ready to go
off and hunt,
no one could
find her.
"I'll see if I
can catch her," said
Vicky's friend, Gal.

Gal, a
Gallimimus,
was the only
dinosaur fast
enough to keep up with Vicky.
"Vicky!" called Gal when
he spotted her. "Your
family is leaving..." But Vicky
was off again.

Much later, Vicky
finally slowed down
and looked around

her. The forest was
empty. "Where is everyone?"
Vicky said, out loud.

"They've gone," said an old voice, and an ancient Protoceratops limped into view. "I saw them go...

...that way."
And Vicky
was off again.

But Vicky was in such a rush, she didn't notice where she was heading. She sped straight into a trap.

That sneaky Protoceratops sent Vicky straight over a cliff!

223

"You won't be eating any of my family tonight," chuckled the Protoceratops, peering down at poor Vicky.

As the old dinosaur ambled away, Gal tried to calm Vicky down a bit.

"Stop flapping!" he shouted over the cliff.

"Slow down and use your claws," suggested Gal.

Another piece of the cliff broke away as Gal encouraged Vicky to keep climbing... slowly.

But once at the top
of the cliff, Vicky sped
off again. "I saw my
family in the valley!
I need to go!" she
told Gal.

"There's a shortcut
through here," she
yelled, and Vicky ran...

...straight into two huge Tarbosaurus!

"Aaaaah!" shrieked Vicky, turning around and racing the other way.

But as she headed deeper into the jungle, Vicky raced into trouble again.

The hanging vines and sticky creepers quickly trapped her, until she was completely tied up.

234

"Stop rushing!" said Gal, when he finally found her. "You're running into trouble at every turn."

Gal helped Vicky escape and led her to a hiding place near the slimy swamp.

"We'll trap the Tarbosaurus in the swamp," said Gal. "Keep shouting so they come closer."

"But why?" asked Vicky. "We could just run past them."

"But we don't want to lead those two pea-brains straight to

your family," replied Gal.
    Both Tarbosaurus were soon
totally tied up and stuck in
the swamp.

A few moments later, Vicky
and Gal emerged from the jungle
and saw Vicky's family further
along the valley. Vicky was
excited to see them again.

"Walk quietly and slowly," said Gal, "or we'll scare away the Protoceratops."

Vicky felt so grateful that Gal had taken the time to help her.

"Being fast is fun," Vicky told the baby Velociraptors. "But it's important to slow down every once in a while, so you don't run into trouble."

Stegosaurus
The thoughtful surprise

Say hello to the dinosaurs in this story!

Stegosaurus
(say *STEG-oh-SORE-us*)

Compsognathus
(say *komp-sog-NATH-us*)

Apatosaurus
(say *ah-PAT-oh-SORE-us*)

Torvosaurus
(say *TOR-voh-SORE-us*)

Juravenator
(say *ju-rah-ve-nay-tor*)

Also featuring: Archaeopteryx
(say *ar-kee-OP-tuh-rix*)

243

There was once a Stegosaurus called Sonny, who lived with his family near a swamp. The family used to live in the forest, but a mean Torvosaurus chased

them from their cave. Sonny
tried not to make a fuss about
moving to a new cave, but he
really missed his
old home.

Sonny was often
so lost in his own
thoughts, he didn't look
where he was going.
"Be careful!" shouted an
angry Compsognathus,
as Sonny almost
flattened him.

Sonny didn't listen properly
either. "Mind the puddle
behind you!" his sister cried,
as Sonny toppled over.

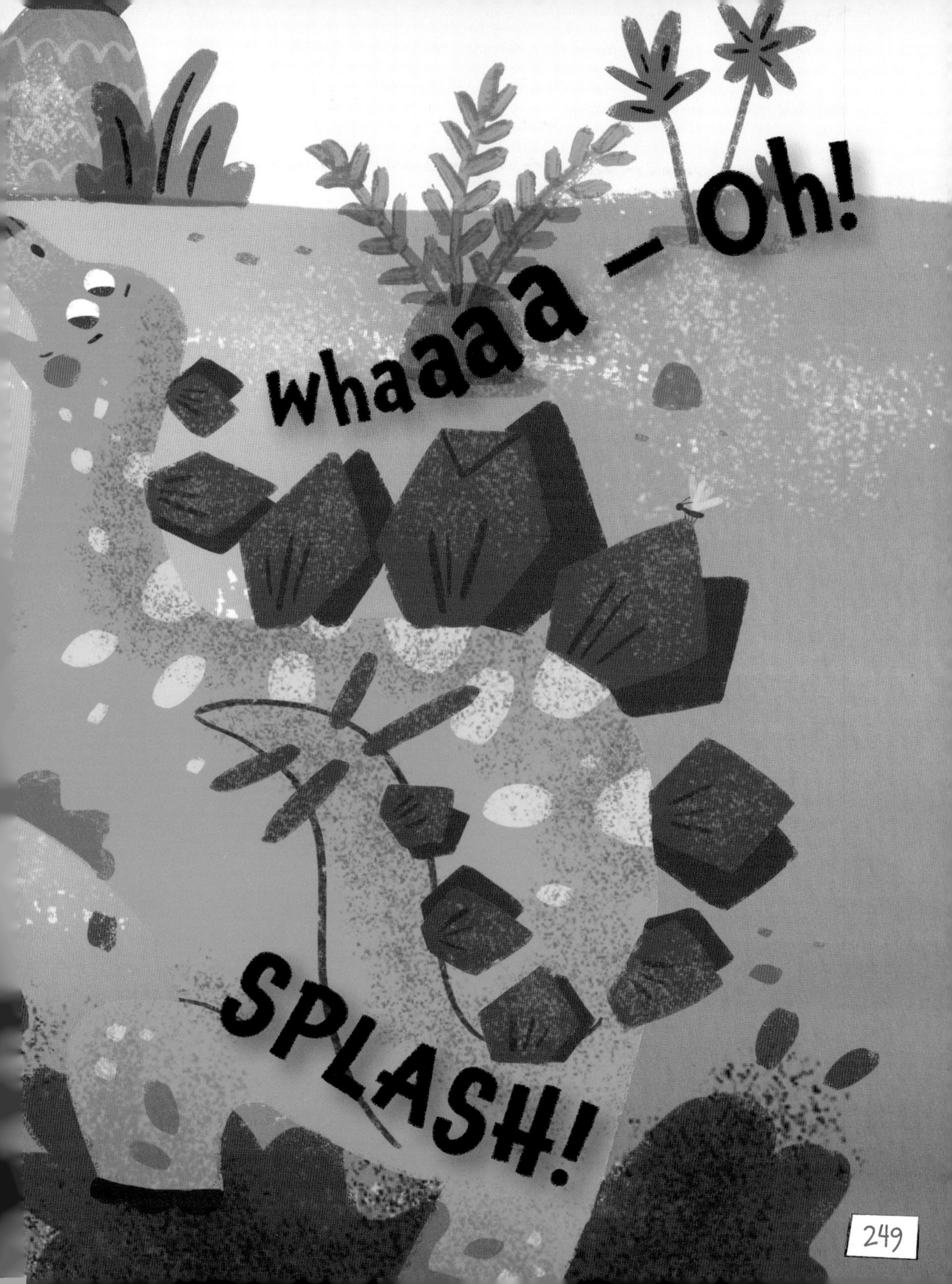
Whaaaa - Oh!
SPLASH!

And Sonny would forget what he was told so often his family thought his ears were stuffed with moss.

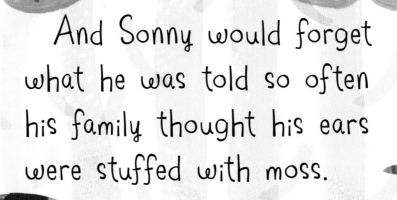

"Remember, don't eat the..." said Sonny's dad.

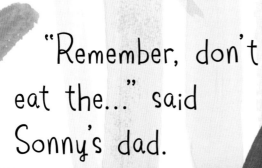

"Ee... urgh!"
spluttered Sonny.
"I forgot that
moss tastes bitter!"

One night Dad said, "What IS it that keeps your mind so busy?" It took a while for Sonny to find the right words.

"I think about LOTS of things," Sonny replied. "Mostly I think about our old home."

"I think about being chased away from our cave. And I think about my old friends,"

he said. "It makes me sad."

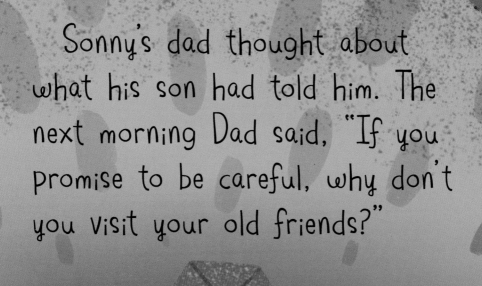

Sonny's dad thought about what his son had told him. The next morning Dad said, "If you promise to be careful, why don't you visit your old friends?"

So Sonny carefully headed back towards his old home. He soon found his friend Ali, an Archaeopteryx.

They spent a lovely morning playing together, but soon it was time to go back home.

As Sonny left, his tail spikes caught a few of Ali's colourful feathers. They stuck to Sonny's tail. But the

friends didn't
notice as they
said goodbye.

Sonny was tired but happy
when he got back to the cave.
"You can go out again tomorrow

as long as you're careful," said Dad, picking the feathers off Sonny's tail.

The next day, Sonny ambled
back through the forest and
found his friend Alina, an
Apatosaurus. Alina was just
about to eat, so they shared
some juicy fern leaves
together.

As Sonny turned to go, he brushed past some more ferns and a few stuck to his back plates. But the friends didn't notice as they said goodbye.

Each time Sonny went out for the day, he came back to the cave a little happier.

"This cave almost feels like home now," said Sonny, as he wandered in to settle down for the night.

The next day, Sonny walked down to the seashore to visit his friend Jag, a Juravenator. At the beach, they dug some huge holes and found some shiny shells.

As Sonny turned to go, his tail swished the

shells. Some flew into the air and landed between Sonny's back plates. But the friends didn't notice as they said goodbye.

But when Sonny got back to the cave, his dad wouldn't let him in. "It's a surprise!" said Dad picking shells off his son. "Give me a few minutes."

Sonny tried to imagine what
his dad might be making...
a dinosaur time machine;
a giant forest funfair?

BANG!
SCRAPE!
CRASH!

came from inside the cave. What was Dad up to?

271

Moments later, Sonny and his sister stood in the middle of their cave with their mouths wide open. Dad had used all the feathers, ferns and shells to decorate the cave. "Every time you visited one of your friends, you came back with something stuck to you!" laughed Dad.

"Our cave looks amazing!" smiled Sonny. "I won't feel so sad now there's something from all of my old friends in my new home."

Allosaurus
The troublesome tooth

Say hello to the dinosaurs in this story!

Allosaurus
(say AL-oh-SORE-us)

Suchomimus
(say sook-oh-MEE-mus)

Nigersaurus
(say nai-jar-sore-us)

Caudipteryx
(say caw-dip-ter-iks)

Once, there was a young Allosaurus called Ava who had a huge mouth full of big, pointy teeth.

Ava was very proud of her teeth.

She was always opening her mouth wide to show them off to her friends.

277

But one day Ava wasn't feeling well, and didn't flash her toothy smile at anyone. "What's wrong?" asked her mum.

"I gok oof ake," mumbled Ava. Poor Ava had toothache and didn't feel like playing with her friends. "I hink I'll sit own under this ush," said Ava.

Not long after, Ava's friend Nina the Nigersaurus dropped by. "Ava, where are you?" cried Nina.

"Urrrrrrrrrr,"
shuddered the bush.
Nina wondered if her
tummy was rumbling.

"Urrrrrrrrr," the noise went again, but louder this time.

"Argh!" screamed Nina. "That bush is alive!" And she trotted off as fast as she could.

Next, Ava's friend Cody the Caudipteryx came looking for her. "Ava!" cried Cody. "Can you come out to play?"

"Ooooooow," shook the bush.

Cody thought the noise must be the wind blowing through the bushes.

"Ooooooow," it went again, but much louder this time.

"Yikes!" screamed Cody. "That bush is alive!"

And he ran away as fast as he could.

A bit later, Shay the Suchomimus walked past the bush, looking for Ava. "Grrrrrrrrr!" the bush rattled.

Shay thought the noise might be a monster. "Grrrrrrrrrr," came the noise again, and the bush started to move. "Help!" screamed Shay. "That bush is alive and it's coming after me!"

The bush monster shuddered
and shook as it ran after Shay.
Then as flowers and leaves fell
off, Ava appeared.

"Ick's me!" spluttered Ava, "I nok a mon ser!" Nina and Cory rushed to where all the noise was coming from.

294

Ava told her friends that she had crawled under the bush because of her toothache.

"Try chewing on a gingko leaf," said Nina. "That helps me."

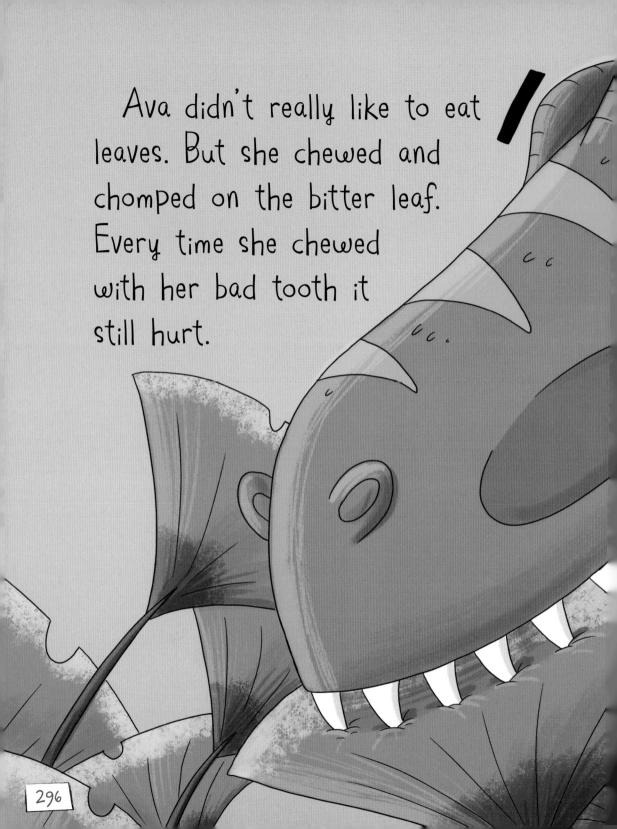

Ava didn't really like to eat leaves. But she chewed and chomped on the bitter leaf. Every time she chewed with her bad tooth it still hurt.

"Try gargling
with water,"
said Cody.

And he dipped an empty
shell in a puddle
and filled it
with the
cool water.

299

Ava gargled and
swished the water
round in her mouth.
"Ick's still nok wor...
king," sighed Ava.

301

Shay was hunting for something on the leafy ground. "Ah, found one!" he said, and he held up a big bone. "Try crunching on that!"

Ava crunched and crushed the bone.

But every time she bit on the side of her poorly tooth, it hurt.

CRACK! CRUNCH!

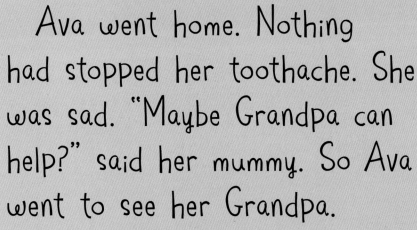

Ava went home. Nothing had stopped her toothache. She was sad. "Maybe Grandpa can help?" said her mummy. So Ava went to see her Grandpa.

Ava told Grandpa everything she had tried to cure her toothache...

She had chewed a gingko
leaf... gargled with cold water...
and even crunched on a bone.

"Open wide," said Grandpa. Grandpa almost put his whole nose in Ava's mouth to get a good look at her bad tooth.

"Go home and try to sleep," said Grandpa. "I think that tooth may fix itself very soon," he said.

The next morning as Ava
opened her mouth wide to check
her bad tooth, out it popped!
"My toothache has gone!"
beamed Ava. "And soon I will
have a shiny, new tooth!"

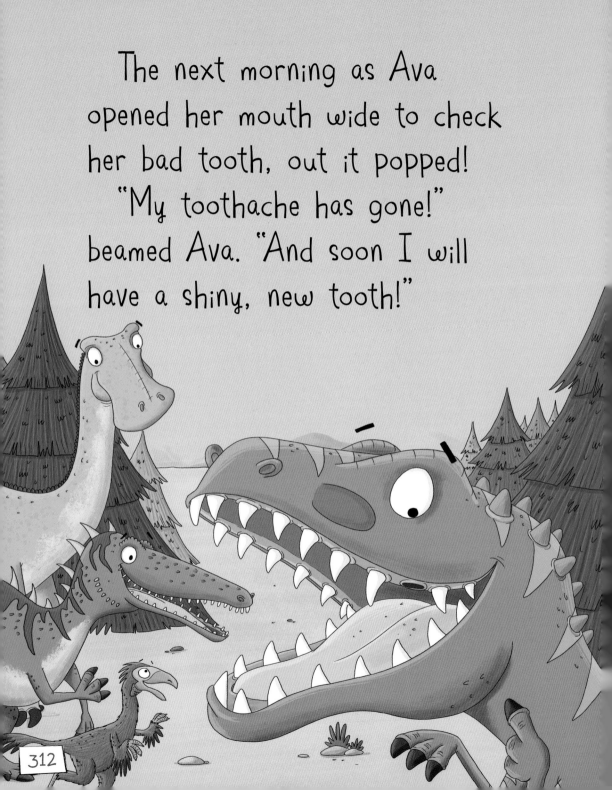

Brachiosaurus

The nosy dinosaur

Say hello to the dinosaurs in this story!

Brachiosaurus
(say *BRAK-ee-oh-sore-us*)

Brachytrachelopan
(say *brak-i-trak-eh-loh-pan*)

Podokesaurus
(say *po-doh-kee-sore-us*)

Yandusaurus
(say *yan-doo-sore-us*)

Also featuring: Megalosaurus (say *MEG-uh-low-sore-us*)

313

Millions of years ago, huge dinosaurs with very long necks feasted on forest leaves. Bobby the Brachiosaurus wasn't fully grown yet, but he still

had a very, very long neck.
Bobby's favourite thing to do
was stretch his long neck as
far as it would go and be as
nosy as possible!

One day, Bobby was munching on leaves as usual when Posy the Podokesaurus rushed by, carrying some moss in her mouth.

"What are you
doing, Posy?"
Bobby asked.

317

But Posy had disappeared behind a bush. And because Bobby was nosy, he stretched his looooong neck over the bush to see where Posy had gone. "Bobby! You've woken my babies!" cried Posy.

Bobby went back to munching leaves, but it wasn't long before he heard a loud snore coming from behind a rock.

"Who's there?"
Bobby asked, but
no one answered.

ZZZzz!

Bobby stretched his very long
neck to peep behind the rock.
He gently nudged a snoring
dinosaur. "What are you doing?"
grumbled a grumpy
Brachytrachelopan
called Ben.

Bobby's day was not going well. He was feeling a bit sorry for himself when he saw

a group of Yandusaurus playing tag. 'That looks fun!' thought Bobby, so he set off after them.

The Yandusaurus zipped through the forest. They were much smaller and speedier than Bobby.

They leapt over logs, skidded round trees and squeezed under branches, until...

...Bobby lost them. He stretched out his long neck to look around.

He was about to give
up and go home when he
heard some giggling from
behind a clump of trees.

What was so funny?
Bobby needed to know!

He used his long neck to puuuuuush his head through the branches to get a better look.

As Bobby's head and neck squeezed through, he saw the Yandusaurus throwing leaves over each other. Bobby laughed and one of them spotted him.

"Hey, what are you doing, nosy?" cried Yasmina, the eldest Yandusaurus. Then in the distance there came a loud, "ROARRRR!"

"Megalosaurus! RUN!" shouted Yasmina.

ROARRRRR!

But Bobby's head and neck were stuck fast between the tree branches! "HELP!" cried Bobby. "My head's stuck!"

The Yandusaurus sped back to help. They climbed on top of each other until they'd made a tall tower. Then the littlest Yandusaurus at the top pushed Bobby's head, hard.

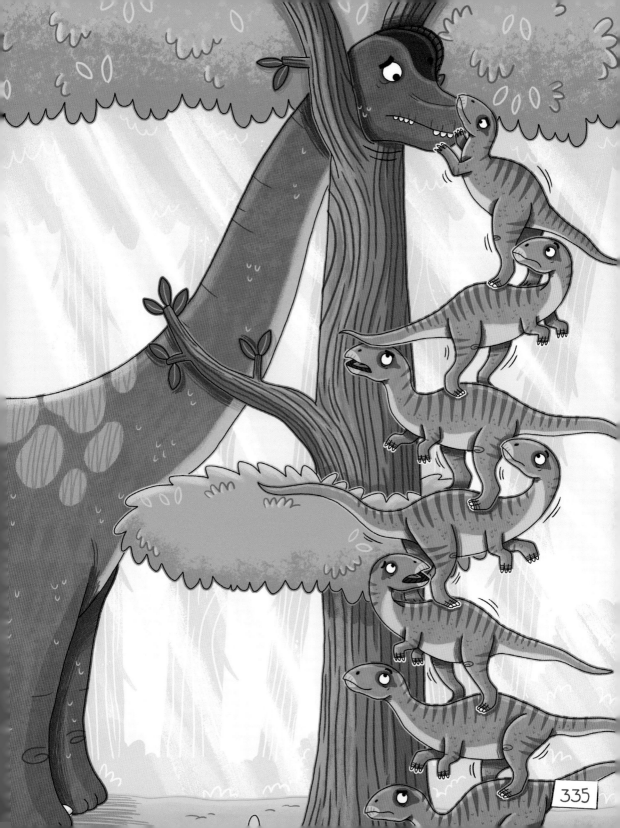

But the Yandusaurus weren't strong enough to push Bobby out. Old Ben heard all the noise and came to help. "Let's try pulling Bobby out," he said.

So the Yandusaurus and Ben
all grabbed hold of Bobby's tail.
"One...two...three...PUUULLL!"

All the dinosaurs pulled as hard as they could. But Bobby was still stuck fast. "Again!" yelled Ben. And he pulled so hard he toppled backwards.

Luckily, the little Yandusaurus managed to scramble out of the way before being squashed. Suddenly, Posy arrived with her babies.

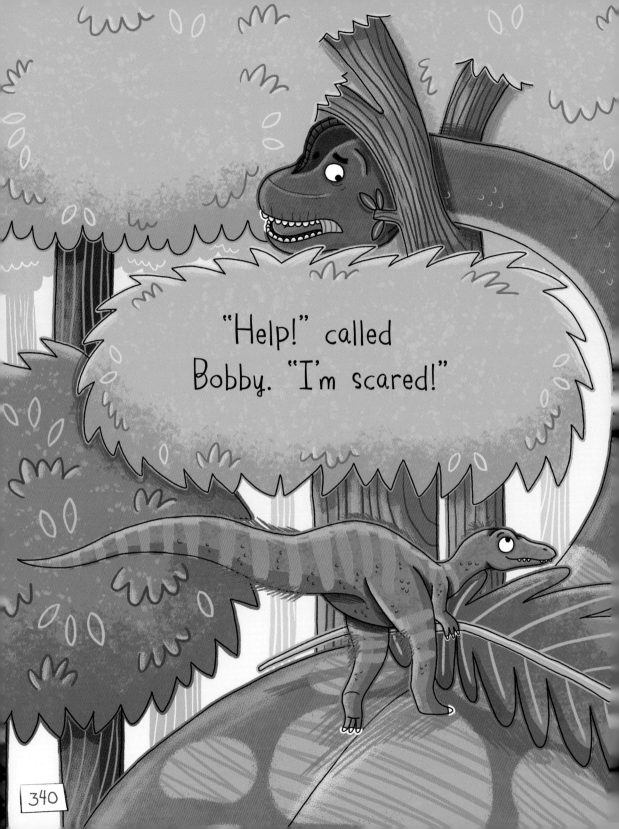

Then Pablo, one of the Podokesaurus babies, had an idea. He grabbed a big leaf and scrambled along Bobby's back.

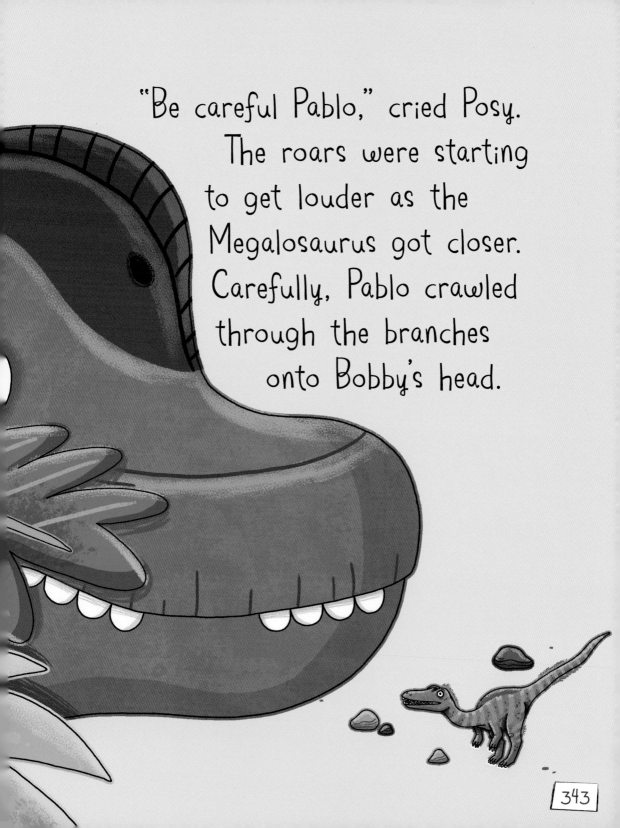

"Be careful Pablo," cried Posy.
The roars were starting
to get louder as the
Megalosaurus got closer.
Carefully, Pablo crawled
through the branches
onto Bobby's head.

"I'm not sure how you can help with that leaf, little one," said Bobby.

"I may be small, but wait and see," said Pablo. Then he tickled Bobby's nose with the leaf! "AAAA...TISH...OOOOO!" Bobby sneezed so hard, his head shot out from between the branches. He was out!

"It's good to be curious," said Ben as they all ran away. "But always check before poking your nose into things!" And the Megalosaurus was something Bobby did NOT want to find out about!

Iguanodon

The noisy night

Say hello to the dinosaurs in this story!

Iguanodon
(say *ig-WHA-noh-don*)

Sauropelta
(say *SORE-oh-pel-tah*)

Amargasaurus
(say *ah-MAR-ga-SORE-us*)

Rebbachisaurus
(say *re-bash-i-SORE-us*)

Also featuring: Liaoxiornis (say *lawh-si-OR-nis*)

347

One stormy night, millions of years ago, an Iguanodon called Isaac could not sleep. Thunder cracked, lightning fizzed and heavy rain hammered onto the rocks. His herd

dozed peacefully, but the noisy night kept Isaac awake.

CHOMP CHOMP CHOMP!

At last, the storm quietened and Isaac was just dropping off to sleep, when...

Amos the Amargasaurus was having a midnight snack!

"Please be quiet!" Isaac shouted. "Night is not the time for snacking!"

And Isaac stuck a fir cone in each ear to block out the noise.

Amos stopped eating
and Isaac was just
nodding off again,
when...

Now Ruksana the
Rebbachisaurus was
having a bad dream.

"Shush!" Isaac called out, louder this time. "Night is not the time for shouting!"

And Isaac lay down again and pulled a big palm leaf over his face.

Ruksana settled down and Isaac was drifting off for a third time, when...

SCRITCH! SCRITCH! SCRATCH!

A Sauropelta called Stanley was scratching an itch between his shoulder spikes!

"STOP!" yelled Isaac
as loud as he could.
"Night is not the time
for scratching!" And
he buried his head
under his mum's leg.

SSSSSSSSS

Suddenly there was an enormous CRACK! from the storm again and Isaac jumped. He squeezed in between his mum and dad, and next to his little sister.

But maybe that wasn't such a good idea either...

"ZZZZzzzzzzzz," snored his dad. "SSSSSsssssss," went his mum. And "EEEEeeeeeee," wheezed his baby sister.

Just about everything else in
the forest that could make a
noise did make a noise that
night. When would it ever end!

Thunder boomed.
BOOOOOOOM!
Trees creaked.
CCCRRREEEAAAK!

Wind howled.
OOOOO-EEEE!

BBBUUUZZZ!

Even the bugs buzzed
louder than usual.
"BE QUIET!" Isaac yelled
at it all.

The next day, Isaac came up with a plan. He collected pine nuts, horsetail plants, fern leaves and all of the things that Amos loved to eat.

Then he took all
the food to Amos.
"Here's a big
feast for you

to eat before bedtime," said
Isaac. "Then you won't snack in
the night."

Next, Isaac rushed around the forest looking for unusual

creatures. He soon spotted a lovely Liaoxiornis.

Isaac wanted to tell Ruksana a relaxing story to help her settle for the night.

Isaac made up a super story about the Liaoxiornis. "I'll tell you the ending at bedtime," he

said to Ruksana.
"You'll have happy, sleepy
thoughts tonight,"
Isaac promised.

There wasn't much time left. Isaac rushed back into the forest and looked for a special piece of rough and bumpy bark.

Isaac found just what he was looking for and took it back for Stanley.

"This will be perfect for you to scratch your back on before bedtime," he told Stanley.

It was getting dark, but Isaac was still busy. He tied back loose branches and...

...blocked gaps in any trees that might whistle in the wind.

He slapped moss on any rocks
that might be noisy if it rained...

...and made a cosy palm leaf
tent to sleep under.

Then Isaac tripped over something in the dull evening light. He looked down at two palm leaf bulbs poking out from the ground. They were the perfect size to block his ears!

"Phew!" sighed Isaac, trying the palm leaf bulbs in his ears. "That busy day has tired me out. I'll just sit here for a while."

By bedtime the forest was quiet, but no one could find Isaac.

His friends searched the forest and found Isaac asleep behind a tree. Now the only sound anyone could hear was Isaac snoring, very loudly!

ZZZZZZZ!